TO QUELA, MY SISTER

Visit us on the Web! www.randomhouse.com/kids

Educators and librarians, for a variety of teaching tools,
visit us at www.randomhouse.com/teachers

Library of Congress Cataloging-in-Publication Data
Piven, Hanoch.
My best friend is as sharp as a pencil : and other funny classroom portraits / Hanoch Piven.—1st ed.
p. cm.
Summary: When her grandma asks her about school, a girl draws a class portrait,
adding details that show what makes each person special.
ISBN 978-0-375-85338-8 (trade) — ISBN 978-0-375-95629-4 (glb)
[1. Portraits—Fiction. 2. Schools—Fiction. 3. Individuality—Fiction.] I. Title.
PZ7.P68943Mw 2010
[E]—dc22
2009025064

The text of this book is set in Apollo.
The illustrations are rendered in gouache on paper adorned with glued-on objects.
Photography by Cristina Reche
Book design by Rachael Cole

MANUFACTURED IN CHINA

2 4 6 8 10 9 7 5 3 1

First Edition

My Best Friend is as Sharp as a Pencil

AND OTHER FUNNY CLASSROOM PORTRAITS BY HANOCH PIVEN

schwartz & wade books · new york

When Grandma comes to visit, she asks so many questions about school.

What is your teacher like?

What's your favorite part of the day?

Who is your best friend?

Who is your favorite teacher?

Who do you play with?

Who is your second-best friend?

Who's in your class?

This time, instead of giving her the same old boring answers, I have an idea. . . .

I'll show her!

Now, Grandma, let's see. You asked about my teacher, Mrs. Jennings.

 Mrs. Jennings talks in a voice as sweet as candy

(except when she is very excited).

She can spell anything, without making one mistake!

 And she smells soooo lovely—as lovely as flowers.

But you gotta be careful: she notices everything, just like a pair of glasses.

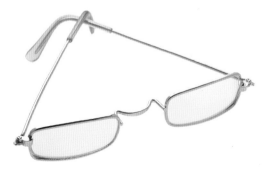

Mrs. Jennings,
I am giving you an A$^+$!

At recess I like to play
with my best friend, Jack.

Jack knows everything about every country in the world.

Jack is as sharp as a pencil,

as curious as a magnifying glass,

and as precise as a microscope.

Is he a genius, or what?!

It will take me about 1,200 steps to cross the smallest country in the world—the Vatican!

What is the most fun part about school? Going to the library!

(See? I'm smart, too.)

Listening to Mrs. Sheila,
the librarian, is as exciting as
rubbing a magic lamp.

She is as interesting as
a book full of stories.

When she reads them, her
eyes shine like marbles.

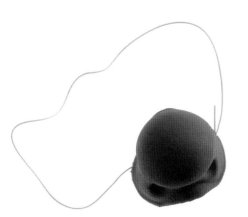

She can be as funny as
a clown

or as scary as
a monster.

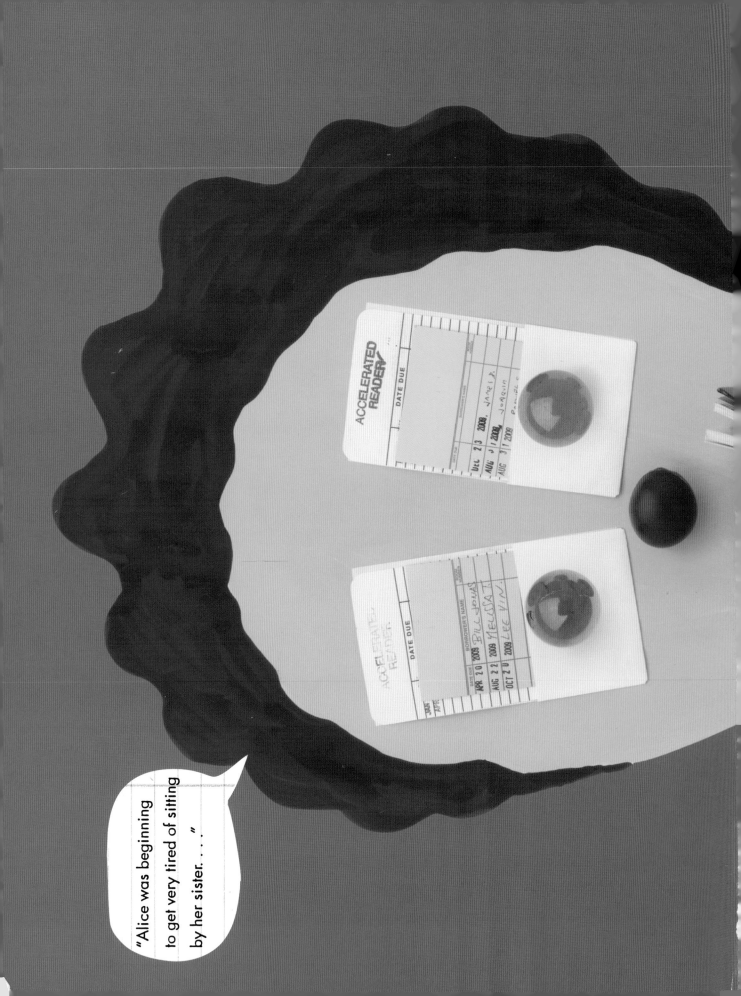

Shhhhhh!
There's a story
starting now!

And who is my
favorite teacher?

My favorite teacher is as mysterious as dark glasses

and as artistic as a paint palette.

He's as relaxed as my favorite pair of jeans

and always so colorful, just like my new set of crayons.

He is Mr. Christoph,
my art teacher.

(Isn't he cool?)

There is one person
in my school
who is so much fun!

She is as happy as a balloon,

as graceful as a ballet slipper,

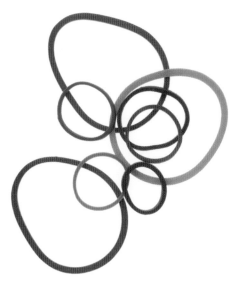

as jumpy as a million
rubber bands,

and as loud as
jingling bells.

She is . . .
She is . . .

Sofia

(the wildest girl in my class).

It's PARTY TIME!

My second-best friend
in school is someone
very quiet.

Someone who is slower than a snail.

Someone who is as hard as a nut

(and has a shell, too),

someone as green as lettuce leaves.

Can you guess who it is?

Mildred, the turtle
(our class pet).

There are so many
other kids in my class.

One is as playful as a bowling pin,

and one is as smart as a computer part.

One is as happy as gummy worms,

and one is as fancy as lipstick.

One is as loud as a kazoo,

and one is as quiet as a fish.

One is as strong as a bulldozer,

and one is as delicate as the sound of a violin.

Then there's one girl (who looks a lot like me) who is as clever as LEGOs.

I can't show them all to you, but . . .

Here are just a few.
(Can you tell which one is me?)

Does that answer all your questions, Grandma?

A LITTLE AFTERTHOUGHT

During the past ten years, I've visited many schools in the United States and other countries, including Guatemala, Brazil, Israel, Spain, Costa Rica, and Argentina.

In each school, once I showed the children my object art, they immediately got to work. They all made the most magnificent pictures using objects they had collected ahead of time.

I noticed that making collages with objects helps kids (and grown-ups) realize that they can create art even if they are insecure about their artistic abilities.

More important, making pictures out of objects helps to tell stories that might be too long, difficult, or boring told in just words.

Gather as many old and unused objects as you can and start playing with them. Before long, you'll find yourself making art.

—Hanoch Piven